SUPER DC HEROES

SUPERMAN

UNDER THE RED SUN

WRITTEN BY
BLAKE A. HOENA

ILLUSTRATED BY
DAN SCHOENING

SUPERMAN CREATED BY
JERRY SIEGEL AND
JOE SHUSTER

P00760
JF
HOF

 www.raintreepublishers.co.uk
Visit our website to find out
more information about
Raintree books.

Phone 0845 6044371
Fax +44 (0) 1865 312263
Email myorders@capstonepub.co.uk

Customers from outside the UK please telephone +44 1865 312262

Raintree is an imprint of Capstone Global Library Limited,
a company incorporated in England and Wales having its registered office at
7 Pilgrim Street, London, EC4V 6LB – Registered company number: 6695582

"Raintree" is a registered trademark of Pearson Education Limited, under licence to
Capstone Global Library Limited

First published by Stone Arch Books in 2009
First published in hardback in the United Kingdom in 2010
Paperback edition first published in the United Kingdom in 2010
The moral rights of the proprietor have been asserted.

Art Director: Bob Lentz
Designer: Bob Lentz
UK Editor: Vaarunika Dharmapala
Originated by Capstone Global Library Ltd
Printed and bound in China by Leo Paper Products Ltd

ISBN 978 1 406214 89 5 (hardback)
14 13 12 11 10
10 9 8 7 6 5 4 3 2 1

ISBN 978 1 406215 03 8 (paperback)
14 13 12 11 10
10 9 8 7 6 5 4 3 2 1

British Library Cataloguing in Publication Data
A full catalogue record for this book is available from the British Library.

CONTENTS

CHAPTER 1

A STRANGE SIGHTING

The newsroom of the *Daily Planet* was busy, as usual. Reporters yelled to each other from across the room. Photographers dashed in and out. Keyboards clicked rapidly. Printers hummed, and phones rang throughout the office.

Only one thing could quiet the madness. That was Perry White, editor-in-chief. He ran Metropolis's most respected newspaper. When his office door opened, everyone in the newsroom stopped what they were doing and listened.

"Clark," Perry barked. "I've got a lead for you."

Reporter Clark Kent looked up from his desk. "What is it, Mr White?" he asked.

"Scientists at the observatory say they've spotted something unusual," Perry replied. "This sounds right up your alley. You're always digging up stories on Superman. Maybe it's another alien heading to Earth."

"I'm on it," Clark said.

Clark jumped to his feet. Then, grabbing a pad of paper, he headed for the door. Behind him, Perry's voice boomed. "Why are the rest of you standing around?!" he shouted. "We've got a paper to run!"

As he exited the building, Clark bumped into Jimmy Olsen. Jimmy worked as a photographer for the *Daily Planet*.

"Where're you headed?" Jimmy asked.

"To the observatory outside town," Clark replied.

"Any chance you need some pictures taken?" Jimmy asked. "I was supposed to photograph the new polar bear cub at the zoo. But my flash frightened it. Now the little guy won't come out of his den."

"There's just going to be telescopes and astronomers," Clark said. "Nothing too exciting."

"Please!" Jimmy begged. "If I don't bring back something, Mr White's going to have me working in the post room again."

"Fine," Clark gave in. "Come on."

Clark hailed a cab, and then they were on their way, zooming down the busy streets of Metropolis.

Nearly an hour later, Clark and Jimmy arrived at their destination. The observatory was a tall, round building with a domed roof. A large telescope poked out of an opening in the roof. It was pointed towards the sun.

Once inside, Clark and Jimmy were led to the telescope room. There, astronomer Gail Perkins and an assistant greeted them.

"We're so glad you could make it," Gail beamed. "You won't believe what we've discovered."

"Can I look?" Jimmy pointed at the telescope's eyepiece.

"No," Gail stopped him. "Looking at the sun through a telescope would blind you."

"Jimmy," Clark cautioned. "Just take pictures."

"But all that's here," Jimmy complained, "are telescopes and astronomers. Nothing too exciting."

Clark rolled his eyes.

"To view the sun safely," Gail explained, "we display it there."

She pointed to a large monitor on a wall of the observatory. Her assistant flipped a switch. On the screen appeared a large, yellowish-orange orb.

Clark walked over to the monitor and squinted. "There's something near the sun."

"You're very observant, Mr Kent," Gail exclaimed. She walked over to the monitor and pointed out a small, blurry splotch, hardly visible to the naked eye. "We're actually surprised we noticed it against the sun's brightness."

"So what is it?" Jimmy asked.

"Probably a stray asteroid," Gail replied. "We need to observe it a little longer before we know for sure. I was hoping it'd drift out into space. Then we could view it better. But oddly, it's staying directly between Earth and the sun."

Hmmmm, that is odd, Clark thought to himself. *I need to get a closer look.*

"Jimmy," Clark said. "Why don't you have Ms Perkins and her assistant show you around the observatory? And make sure you take some pictures!"

"What are you going to do, Mr Kent?" Jimmy asked.

Clark pulled a notepad and a pencil from his pocket. "I need to jot down some notes," he said. "Then I'll catch up."

As soon as everyone left the room, Clark walked over to the telescope's eyepiece. He ignored the astronomer's warnings. Without thinking twice, Clark bent down to look through the eyepiece.

Anyone else would have been blinded by the sun's intense rays, but Clark Kent had a secret. He was also Superman, the Man of Steel. Clark was unharmed by the sun's brightness. In fact, it was the yellow rays of the sun that gave him his superpowers.

With his super-vision and the magnification of the telescope, he could clearly see the object near the sun, and it wasn't an asteroid. It looked more like a giant necklace with hundreds of shiny, metal beads.

"It's some sort of spaceship," Clark said quietly to himself.

Clark knew he needed to find out more about the object. Professor Emil Hamilton would be able to help. He worked at the Scientific and Technological Advanced Research Laboratories, also known as S.T.A.R. Labs. The Professor had developed a spacesuit, which Superman used to fly in outer space.

Quickly, Clark found Jimmy. "But I didn't get a chance to take any pictures," Jimmy complained as Clark led him outside.

They hopped in the cab and headed back to Metropolis.

CHAPTER 2

KALIBAK

On the dark side of the moon, a brilliant flash lit up the sky. It was followed by a thunderous **KA-BOOM!** Suddenly, a spaceship appeared out of nowhere.

At the ship's helm sat Kalibak, a large, hulking beast. He was the eldest son of one of Superman's enemies, Darkseid. Kalibak's father ruled the faraway planet Apokolips.

The view screen in front of Kalibak displayed a small man named Desaad. He was an evil scientist who worked for Darkseid.

"Once you activate the Solar Net," Desaad explained to Kalibak, "it will block the yellow rays of Earth's sun. Superman will be weakened. Helpless."

"Your invention had better work," Kalibak growled. "I risk my father's wrath by trusting you."

"My inventions always work," Desaad sneered.

Kalibak flipped a switch on his ship's control panel. The object that Gail Perkins had spotted suddenly came to life. Its shiny bead-like pods began to spread, forming an enormous circle directly between Earth and the sun.

"It's ready," Kalibak stated.

"Then what are you waiting for?" screeched Desaad.

"By trusting you, I am disobeying my father," Kalibak explained. "He forbade anyone from attacking Earth until his plans to defeat Superman were complete."

"But think of the glory," Desaad grinned. "If you defeat Superman, nothing can stop Darkseid from conquering Earth. You'll be a hero."

"I will make my father proud," Kalibak mumbled to himself.

He flipped another switch. Then the pods began emitting red laser beams. Each pod shot out hundreds of beams, with each of the beams connecting it to one of the other pods. By the time all the pods were connected, the beams formed a large net of light – a Solar Net. Sunlight shining towards Earth turned red as it passed through the Solar Net.

Back on Earth, a cab dropped off Jimmy and Clark at the Daily Planet. Jimmy skipped up the steps to the front door. At the top, he turned around to see if Clark was following. He was nowhere to be seen.

Huh? Jimmy thought. *I wonder where Clark ran off to.*

While standing there, Jimmy noticed something strange above him. The sun flickered, changing from yellow to red.

Now that's odd, Jimmy thought.

As soon as he got out of the cab, Clark had ducked around the corner. He then ran down an alley, looking for a secluded spot. Once he knew that he was alone, he shed his shirt and tie. He changed into Superman, wearing a bright blue suit with a red "S" on his chest.

Superman planned to head to S.T.A.R. Labs. Then, after donning his special spacesuit, he could investigate the object near Earth's sun.

Leaping into the air, Superman noticed a plume of smoke billowing from the top floors of a skyscraper. *I'd better make sure no one is in danger,* he thought to himself. Listening with his super-hearing, Superman heard a frantic cry for help.

WHOOOOSH!

Faster than a speeding bullet, he zipped off towards the sound of danger.

A frightened woman had crawled on to a window ledge. She was trying to escape the flames inside the building. Superman swooped down and scooped her up. She was as light as a feather in his arms.

Just then, the sunlight turned from the normal yellow colour that gave Superman his power to a reddish hue. Superman felt weak. The woman grew heavy in his arms. He felt the tug of gravity and began to fall.

As he fell, Superman wrapped his arms around the woman to protect her. They crashed to the pavement below. WHAM!

Once the dust cleared, the woman could be seen safely sitting on Superman's chest.

"Are you okay?" he groaned.

"It looks like I should be asking you that," the woman replied.

Superman tried to sit up. "I'll be fine," he said. "But could you please get up?"

The woman quickly stood up and helped Superman to his feet. Everyone around them was staring in awe at Earth's red sun.

Meanwhile, in the darkness of space, Kalibak watched his Solar Net in action. "It appears to be working," Kalibak said. "But solar flares are causing it to flicker. Some of the sun's yellow rays are getting through."

"A small matter. Superman will still be weakened," Desaad sneered. "Now is the time for you to attack!"

"Let me test him first," Kalibak snickered.

He pressed a button, and a hatch opened on the bottom of his ship. From the opening emerged three soldiers, hideous warriors from Apokolips.

They roared their battle cry and then flew towards Earth, claws glinting menacingly in the red sunlight.

CHAPTER 3

SUPERMAN IN TROUBLE

Superman felt woozy and sore. His back ached, and his head pounded. He wasn't used to feeling so much pain after a fall. Actually, Superman wasn't used to falling from the sky.

He looked up at the red sun. Its rays didn't fill his body with energy – not like the yellow rays of sunlight had. He didn't feel as strong as he normally did. The red rays of light were robbing him of his superpowers.

"What are those?" someone near Superman yelled. Three greenish blurs streaked through the sky. They were honing in on Superman.

Soldiers from Apokolips, Superman thought to himself. *That must mean . . .*

But he didn't have time to finish his thought. All three monsters crashed into him. Superman and the creatures rolled down the street in a ball of flailing arms and legs. People screamed and jumped out of the way. Then Superman and the monsters crashed into a building. Bricks fell everywhere, thudding to the ground.

Before Superman could recover, one of the creatures lifted Superman over its head and tossed him into a building on the other side of the street. WHAM!

One of the other creatures walked up to Superman and slugged him across the jaw. **KRAK!** Superman was sent flying down the block, and then laid in the middle of the street, groaning in pain.

The third creature picked up a car. He slammed it down on Superman again and again. **SMASH! SMASH!**

Thinking that Superman was so easily defeated, the evil monsters turned to attack the helpless bystanders. People ran and screamed as the creatures lurched toward them.

From underneath the car, Superman heard the screams and feared what would happen to the people. He was weakened, but he was not without some of his superpowers. Through sheer will, Superman stood up, lifting the car over his head.

When Superman finally got up, the monsters spotted him. Roaring ferociously, they charged at Superman, their claws whirling through the air. Superman ducked and dodged. His fists slammed into jaws and chests.

The creatures snarled and snorted angrily. Superman fought bravely, but he was outnumbered and weakened. Soon, the creatures had him surrounded. He retreated down an alley until he was backed up against a building.

One of the creatures lunged, grabbing Superman by the arm. Another grabbed his other arm. They pinned him against a wall.

The third evil creature walked up to Superman, chuckling. He pulled his fist back and then slammed it into Superman's jaw. **KA-POW!** Superman fell to his knees.

Millions of miles away, a solar flare erupted from the sun, sending a burst of energy and yellow sunlight out into space. It streaked towards Earth, causing Desaad's Solar Net to flicker. Some of the yellow sunlight escaped through the net and reached Earth.

Superman felt the energy from the yellow rays of sunlight coarse through his body. He felt some of his strength return.

As the creature prepared to strike him again, Superman mustered up all of his strength. He lifted the two creatures holding his arms off the ground.

Then Superman clapped his hands together. All three evil monsters slammed into each other. WHAM! They crashed to the ground and lay there motionless.

Down the alley, a cab screeched to a halt. Jimmy Olsen jumped out, readying his camera.

"I've got to get some pictures of those things!" Jimmy exclaimed.

Superman rushed past Jimmy. He headed towards the cab.

"Where are you going?" Jimmy asked.

"I need to get to S.T.A.R. Labs," Superman replied, getting into the cab.

Jimmy jumped into the seat behind him. "Wouldn't it be quicker to fly?" he asked.

Superman looked up at Earth's red sun. The solar flare was over. He couldn't feel any yellow rays of sunlight shining down on him.

"Not this time," he said.

CHAPTER 4

S.T.A.R. LABS

At S.T.A.R. Labs, Professor Emil Hamilton greeted Superman and Jimmy. They were surprised to see astronomer Gail Perkins there as well.

"I came over to S.T.A.R. Labs as soon as I noticed a change in the object," Gail began. "It appears to be some sort of spaceship designed to filter the sun's rays."

"Has it affected you?" Emil asked.

"It's robbed me of most of my powers," Superman replied. "I can't even fly."

"How can we stop it?" Jimmy asked.

Emil flipped on a monitor. The screen displayed a map of the solar system, showing the Solar Net between Earth and the sun. Several blinking lights also appeared on the screen.

"Those lights represent Earth's satellite defence system," explained Emil.

He flipped on a second monitor that showed one of the satellites. A hatch opened as a rocket launched.

"The satellites are targeting the Solar Net," Emil said.

On the first monitor, several streaks of light could be seen heading towards the Solar Net. As they neared their target, Kalibak's spaceship appeared from its hiding spot on the dark side of the moon.

Kalibak's spaceship shot out several beams of light, and one by one, the rockets were destroyed. Then the spaceship attacked and destroyed the satellites.

"What was that?" Jimmy exclaimed.

"That's who's behind all of this," Superman said. "And those monsters that attacked me are from Apokolips. This is the work of Darkseid."

"How can we stop them?" Jimmy asked.

"I have an idea," Superman announced.

CHAPTER 5

A FULL MOON

Superman stood in the cargo bay of a large, military plane. The cargo bay door was open, and Superman looked down at the ground miles below him.

"Ms Perkins," Superman spoke into the headset of his spacesuit. "I'm ready."

"Are you sure this is going to work?" she asked. "That's a long way to fall. Even for Superman."

There was a moment's hesitation.

"In theory, it should," came his reply.

Outside the airplane, night had wrapped the world in darkness, but overhead, the full moon shone brightly.

"The Solar Net is only filtering sunlight that shines directly on Earth," Superman explained. "The Moon lights up in the sky because sunlight shines on it and is reflected towards Earth. The Solar Net is not filtering the sunlight reflecting off the Moon. And since it's a full moon tonight, I'm hoping enough yellow rays of sunlight are reflecting off the Moon to give me the power to fly."

"I hope you're right," Gail said.

"Okay, Superman," Emil broke in. "The plane is about ten miles above Earth. We don't want to go much higher. We might attract the attention of the spaceship that attacked the satellites.

"Are you ready?" Emil asked.

"As I will ever be," Superman replied.

Superman stepped out of the cargo bay door. The plane zoomed away without him. He just stood there, hovering in midair. The Moon appeared huge overhead. From this high up, its brightness was blinding. Superman could feel the rays of yellow light coursing through his body, strengthening him.

"It worked," Superman spoke into his spacesuit's headset.

"Just stay out of the Solar Net's path," Emil warned. "In outer space, it can still rob you of your powers."

Then, faster than a speeding bullet, Superman flew higher and higher, soaring above Earth and into outer space.

Kalibak, watching on his ship's view screen, saw a tiny object leave Earth's atmosphere and fly towards his ship.

Those earthlings are fools, Kalibak thought. *They think another rocket attack can stop me!*

Then Kalibak's eyes narrowed in anger as he recognized what, or who, was flying towards him. "Superman!"

Kalibak flipped a switch, and Desaad appeared on the view screen.

"Your device didn't work," Kalibak screamed. "Superman is headed straight for my ship."

"How can that be?" Desaad muttered. "Find a way to get him between Earth and the Solar Net. He won't be able to survive in outer space without his powers.

As Superman flew towards the ship, it zoomed away. He gave chase. It circled around the Moon. It zipped right, then left, and stayed just out of Superman's reach.

As Superman was about to catch the spaceship, he couldn't move anymore. He just floated in space. To his horror, as he was chasing after the spaceship, he had flown into the path of the Solar Net's red rays. He was helpless.

The spaceship turned around and headed back towards Superman, stopping feet away. A hatch opened, allowing a large ogre-like creature to emerge.

"Kalibak!" Superman sneered. "I should have known."

Kalibak floated over to Superman. He raised a giant fist above his head.

"This is going to be fun," Kalibak said. He smashed his fist down on Superman, sending him spinning backwards.

"Oh, no you don't," Kalibak growled. "You won't get away that easily."

Jet packs in his suit sent Kalibak flying after Superman. When he caught up to Superman, Kalibak grabbed him around the neck with one hand. With his other hand, Kalibak punched Superman. The Man of Steel struck back at Kalibak, but he was no match for the creature.

As they fought, the pair drifted towards the edge of the Solar Net's path. Superman could feel some rays of yellow sunlight reaching him. They didn't give him enough strength to break free from Kalibak's grasp, but he was able to raise his hands to stop the next blow.

Looking over Kalibak's shoulder, Superman could see that they were near one of the pods of the Solar Net. Superman focused his heat-vision on the pod. A second later, it exploded.

"Huh?" Kalibak turned around to see what had happened.

That gave Superman enough time to break free. He aimed his heat-vision at another pod, destroying it.

"No!" Kalibak screamed.

Then another pod exploded. And another.

By time Kalibak reached Superman, several of the pods had been destroyed. The Solar Net was weakening. It couldn't filter out all of the yellow sunlight. Superman was regaining his strength.

Kalibak swung at Superman. The Man of Steel stopped the blow by catching Kalibak's fist in his hand. Then he struck Kalibak, sending him reeling backwards.

"Even with the return of your superpowers," Kalibak growled. "I will still defeat you!"

He charged at Superman.

Just then, a loud boom erupted, separating Kalibak and Superman. A tall, dark figure appeared between them. It was Darkseid!

Fuming with anger, Darkseid turned toward Kalibak.

"You have disobeyed my orders," Darkseid's voiced boomed.

"Father, I'm sorry," Kalibak grovelled. "I just –"

Before Kalibak could finish, two red rays shot out of Darkseid's eyes. They struck Kalibak and enveloped him in light. When the light faded, Kalibak was gone.

Then Darkseid turned to Superman.

"Your time will come, Superman," Darkseid growled. "Until then . . ."

Another loud boom sounded, and Darkseid was gone.

•   •   •

Back at the Daily Planet Building, Clark Kent skipped up the steps. At the top, he saw Jimmy Olsen off to the side, moping.

"What's wrong?" Clark asked.

Jimmy looked up at Clark and gave him a weak grin.

"Well," he began. "With all the excitement, between visiting the observatory, seeing Superman attacked, and going to S.T.A.R. Labs, I forgot to take any pictures. I don't even have one of that polar bear cub. Nothing.

"I suppose it's back to the post room," Jimmy sighed. "At least you took some notes for your story."

Clark walked up to Jimmy and put his arm around his young friend's shoulder. Then he guided Jimmy through the front doors.

"I wasn't with you at S.T.A.R. Labs," Clark said. "You can fill me in on what happened there. We can share credit for the story."

"Really!" Jimmy exclaimed.

"Sure," Clark laughed. "Anything to keep you from losing my post again."

"Maybe I should become a reporter," said Jimmy. "Do you think Mr White will let me?"

"Don't get your hopes up."

WHO IS KALIBAK?

Kalibak is a massive, evil man-beast born on Apokolips, a distant world ruled by his father Darkseid. Kalibak constantly seeks his father's approval, indifferent to those who might be harmed, or killed, in the process. Known for his resilience and strength, Kalibak is capable of standing toe-to-toe with even Superman himself for brief periods of time. He often begins his attacks from afar, weakening his opponents with technology prior to engaging them in hand-to-hand combat.

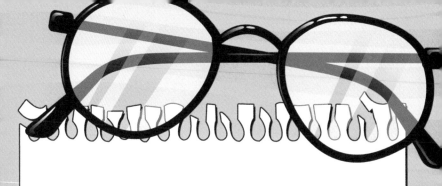

- Kalibak is a known associate of Desaad, Darkseid's leading evil scientist. Both Desaad and Kalibak are dangerous individuals likely to employ deceit whenever it suits them, or when, in Kalibak's case, it may lead to his father's approval.

- As one of Darkseid's sons, Kalibak functions as Darkseid's second-in-command. He often controls Darkseid's flying combat troops.

- Kalibak often uses a melee weapon called the Beta-Club, which causes terrible pain to anyone hit by it.

- Kalibak is an extremely dangerous enemy whose power is matched only by Darkseid and the Man of Steel himself.

- Kalibak uses weapons from Apokolips, where slaves serve their ruler, Darkseid. The sole purpose of the planet is to use slave labour to create weapons of mass destruction. Expect Kalibak to be heavily armed at all times.

BIOGRAPHIES

In his youth, **Blake A. Hoena** wrote stories about robots conquering the Moon and trolls lumbering around in the woods. Since then, Blake has written more than thirty books for children, including a series of graphic novels about two space alien brothers, Eek and Ack, who are determined to conquer Earth.

Dan Schoening has had a passion for animation and comic books from an early age. Currently, Dan does freelance work in the animation and game industry and spends a lot of time with his lovely little daughter, Paige.

GLOSSARY

alien being from another planet

billowing swelling and puffing up

ferocious savage or fierce

filtering separating or blocking part of something

frantic wildly excited by worry or fear

grovel be humble or polite to someone because you are afraid of that person or think he or she is important

honing moving or advancing towards a target or goal

observatory building with telescopes that is used for studying the sky and the stars

solar flare sudden eruption of hydrogen gas on the surface of the sun

theory idea or statement that attempts to explain something logically but cannot be proven

DISCUSSION QUESTIONS

1. Superman has many strengths, but he also has a few weaknesses. What are some of your own strengths and weaknesses?

2. Clark Kent's secret identity is Superman. Why do you think he keeps his alter ego a secret from everyone? Would you tell anybody if you were a super hero?

3. Both Kalibak and Superman use some pretty amazing technology in this story. What's the most impressive scientific device or invention that you've ever seen?

WRITING PROMPTS

1. Imagine that Darkseid has returned to Earth to face off with Superman. Does Superman emerge victorious? What evil plan does Darkseid have in store for the Man of Steel? You decide.

2. Superman has a variety of superpowers like super-strength and super-vision. If you were a super hero, what superpowers would you want? What would you use them for?

3. Kalibak went against his father's orders when he attacked Superman. Have you ever done something you were told not to? What happened? Write about it.